The Berenstain Bears'®
Night Before Christmas

FROM THE POEM BY CLEMENT C. MOORE

'Twas the night before Christmas
in the Bears' tree house home,
when they read of Saint Nicholas
in a beloved old poem.

Mike Berenstain
Based on the characters created by Stan and Jan Berenstain

HARPER FESTIVAL
An Imprint of HarperCollinsPublishers

Copyright © 2013 by Berenstain Publishing, Inc.
Printed in the United States of America. All rights reserved.
No part of this book may be used or reproduced in any manner whatsoever without written permission except in the case of brief quotations embodied
in critical articles and reviews. For information address HarperCollins Children's Books, a division of HarperCollins Publishers, 195 Broadway,
New York, NY 10007.
Library of Congress catalog card number: 2013935049
ISBN 978-0-06-207553-6
21 22   CWM   11 10
❖
First Edition

It was Christmas Eve in the Bear family's tree house, and they were more than ready for a visit from Santa Claus. Their tree was beautifully decorated. Their stockings were carefully hung by the fireplace. Brother, Sister, and Honey even put out a snack of milk and cookies for Santa.

"Good idea!" said Papa. "Sliding down chimneys is hard work. Old Saint Nicholas will be hungry."

"Saint Nicholas?" said Brother. "Who's he?"
"That's an old name for Santa Claus," explained
Mama. "Or he was just called Saint Nick."
"Saint Nick," repeated Sister. "That's cute!"

"There's a famous old poem about him," said Papa, getting a dusty book down from the shelf. "Let's read it together!"

"Actually," said Brother, "we're planning to watch *The Nutty Bears Meet Santa Claus* on TV. It's our Christmas Eve tradition."

The NUTTY Bears

Mama didn't think the Nutty Bears were very Christmasy. All they did was hit one another over the head.

"I think it's time to start a new Christmas Eve tradition," she said firmly. "TV isn't everything. There's such a thing as a plain, old-fashioned book."

Papa opened the book, and the cubs saw its brightly colored pictures. It looked pretty interesting!

"Go ahead and read it, Papa," said Sister.

So Papa began to read "A Visit from Saint Nicholas."

A Visit from Saint Nicholas

"'Twas the night before Christmas, when all
through the house
Not a creature was stirring, not even a mouse;
The stockings were hung by the chimney with care,
In hopes that St. Nicholas soon would be there;

"The children were nestled all snug in their beds,
While visions of sugarplums danced in their heads;

"And Mama in her 'kerchief, and I in my cap,
Had just settled our brains for a long winter's nap,
When out on the lawn there arose such a clatter,
I sprang from the bed to see what was the matter.

"Away to the window I flew like a flash,
Tore open the shutters and threw up the sash.
When what to my wondering eyes should appear,
But a miniature sleigh and eight tiny reindeer,
With a little old driver, so lively and quick,
I knew in a moment it must be St. Nick.

"More rapid than eagles his coursers they came,
And he whistled, and shouted, and called them by name:
'Now, Dasher! Now, Dancer! Now, Prancer and Vixen!
On, Comet! On, Cupid! On, Donder and Blitzen!'
And then, in a twinkling, I heard on the roof
The prancing and pawing of each little hoof.

"As I drew in my head, and was turning around,
Down the chimney St. Nicholas came with a bound.
A bundle of toys he had flung on his back,
And he looked like a peddler just opening his pack.
His eyes—how they twinkled!
His dimples how merry!
His cheeks were like roses, his nose like a cherry!

"He had a broad face and a
little round belly,
That shook when he laughed,
like a bowlful of jelly.
He spoke not a word, but
went straight to his work,

"And filled all the stockings;
then turned with a jerk,
And laying his finger aside of his nose,
And giving a nod, up the chimney he rose.

"He sprang to his sleigh, to his team gave a whistle,
And away they all flew like the down of a thistle,
But I heard him exclaim, ere he drove out of sight,
'Happy Christmas to all, and to all a good night!'"

Papa closed the book. "Well, how did you all like 'A Visit from Saint Nicholas'?" he asked.

"Shhh!" said Mama.
The cubs were all asleep.

Papa and Mama carried the cubs upstairs and nestled them down all snug in their beds.

"Sometimes," said Mama, as they kissed the cubs good night, "there's just nothing like a good book."

They went to bed themselves and settled down for a long winter's nap. The Bear family was ready for their very own visit from Saint Nicholas.

"Happy Christmas to all, and to all a good night!"